Dogs

A Level One Reader

By Cynthia Klingel and Robert B. Noyed

The Child's World®

I love dogs. I want one for a pet.

There are many kinds of dogs.

Some dogs are big.
Some dogs are small.

Most dogs are covered with fur.

Most dogs have a long, furry tail.

Dogs love to run and play outside.

13

Some dogs can learn tricks.

This dog can stand on its rear legs.

18

Most dogs eat special food. It helps them grow strong.

A dog can be a great friend.

Word List

covered

friend

fur

outside

special

tricks

Note to Parents and Educators

Welcome to The Wonders of Reading™! These books provide text at three different levels for beginning readers to practice and strengthen their reading skills. Additionally, the use of nonfiction text provides readers the valuable opportunity to *read to learn*, not just to learn to read.

These leveled readers allow children to choose books at their level of reading confidence and performance. Level One books offer beginning readers simple language, word choice, and sentence structure as well as a word list. Level Two books feature slightly more difficult vocabulary, longer sentences, and longer total text. In the back of each Level Two book are an index and a list of books and Web sites for finding out more information. Level Three books continue to extend word choice and length of text. In the back of each Level Three book are a glossary, an index, and a list of books and Web sites for further research.

State and national standards in reading and language arts emphasize using nonfiction at all levels of reading development. The Wonders of Reading™ fill the historical void in nonfiction material for the primary grade readers with the additional benefit of a leveled text.

About the Authors

Cindy Klingel has worked as a high school English teacher and an elementary teacher. She is currently the curriculum director for a Minnesota school district. Writing children's books is another way for her to continue her passion for sharing the written word with children. Cindy Klingel is a frequent visitor to the children's section of bookstores and enjoys spending time with her many friends, family, and two daughters.

Bob Noyed started his career as a newspaper reporter. Since then, he has worked in communications and public relations for more than fourteen years for a Minnesota school district. He enjoys writing books for children and finds that it brings a different feeling of challenge and accomplishment from other writing projects. He is an avid reader who also enjoys music, theater, traveling, and spending time with his wife, son, and daughter.

Published by The Child's World®, Inc.
PO Box 326
Chanhassen, MN 55317-0326
800-599-READ
www.childsworld.com

Photo Credits
© Alan & Sandy Carey/Tony Stone Images: cover
© Daniel J. Olson/Unicorn Stock Photos: 18
© David Allan Brandt/Tony Stone Images: 6
© Monica Dalmasso/Tony Stone Images: 2
© Myrleen Ferguson/PhotoEdit: 17, 21
© Photri, Inc.: 9
© Renee Lynn/Tony Stone Images: 13
© Sara Gray/Tony Stone Images: 10
© Tim Davis/Tony Stone Images: 5, 14

Project Coordination: Editorial Directions, Inc.
Photo Research: Alice K. Flanagan

Library of Congress Cataloging-in-Publication Data
Klingel, Cynthia Fitterer.
Dogs / by Cynthia Klingel and Robert B. Noyed.
p. cm. — (Wonder books)
Summary: Simple text describes pet dogs, what they can look like,
how they behave, and how to take care of them.
ISBN 1-56766-798-8 (lib. reinforced)
1. Dogs—Juvenile literature. [1. Dogs. 2. Pets.]
I. Noyed, Robert B. II. Title. III. Wonder books (Chanhassen, Minn.)

SF426.5 .K65   2000
636.7—dc21   99-055942